The SUMMER OLYMPICS

ON THE WORLD STAGE

ATHLETES TO WATCH

TOKYO 2020

The SUMMER OLYMPICS

ON THE WORLD STAGE

ATHLETES TO WATCH

FASCINATING FACTS

GREATEST MOMENTS

RECORD BREAKERS

TOKYO 2020

The SUMMER OLYMPICS
ON THE WORLD STAGE

ATHLETES TO WATCH

GREG BACH AND SCOTT MCDONALD

MASON CREST
PHILADELPHIA | MIAMI

MASON CREST

450 Parkway Drive, Suite D, Broomall, Pennsylvania 19008
(866) MCP-BOOK (toll-free) • www.masoncrest.com

First printing

9 8 7 6 5 4 3 2 1
ISBN (hardback) 978-1-4222-4444-9
ISBN (series) 978-1-4222-4443-2
ISBN (ebook) 978-1-4222-7365-4

Library of Congress Cataloging-in-Publication Data

Names: Bach, Greg, author. | McDonald, Scott (Sports journalist) author.
Title: Athletes to watch / Greg Bach and Scott McDonald.
Description: Broomall, Pennsylvania : Mason Crest, [2020] | Series: The summer Olympics: on the world stage | Includes bibliographical references and index.
Identifiers: LCCN 2019038381 | ISBN 9781422244449 (hardback) | ISBN 9781422273654 (ebook)
Subjects: LCSH: Olympic athletes–Juvenile literature. | Olympics–History–Juvenile literature. | Olympic Games–History–Juvenile literature.
Classification: LCC GV721.53 .B33 2020 | DDC 796.48–dc23
LC record available at https://lccn.loc.gov/2019038381

Developed and Produced by National Highlights Inc.
Editor: Andrew Luke
Production: Crafted Content LLC

Cover images, clockwise from top left:

Japanese gymnast Takeru Kitazono (Martin Rulsch@Wikimedia Commons), Tokyo International Exhibition Center, a venue for the 2020 Games (Voyata@Dreamstime.com and Asao Tokolo@Wikimedia Commons), British swimmer Adam Peaty (Fernando Frazao Agencia Brasil@ Wikimedia Commons), USA Track athlete Allyson Felix (jenaragon94@Wikimedia Commons)

QR CODES AND LINKS TO THIRD-PARTY CONTENT

CONTENTS

WHAT ARE THE SUMMER OLYMPICS?

The ancient Olympic Games took place in Greece every four years for nearly 12 centuries from 776 BC through 393 AD. They were part of a religious festival to honor Zeus, who was the father of Greek gods and goddesses. The event was held in Olympia, a sanctuary site named for Mount Olympus, which is the country's tallest mountain and the mythological home of the Greek gods. It is the place for which the Olympics are named.

Roughly 1,500 years after the ancient Games ended, a Frenchman named Baron Pierre de Coubertin wanted to resurrect the Olympic Games to coincide with the 1900 World Fair in Paris. The 1900 Paris Exposition was to feature the newest, modern-day, turn-of-the-century attractions like talking films, the diesel engine, escalators, magnet audio recorders, and a fairly new Eiffel Tower painted yellow.

De Coubertin wanted the best athletes in the world for the first modern Olympic Games outside of Greece, so he presented the idea in 1894. Representatives from 34 potential countries got so excited about his plan that they proposed the Games take place in 1896 instead. So, the modern Olympics, as it is now called, began where the ancient Games left off—in Athens, Greece, in 1896.

The 10-day event in April 1896 had 241 male athletes from 14 countries competing in 43 events. The events at these Athens Games were athletics (track and field), swimming, cycling, fencing, gymnastics, shooting, tennis, weightlifting, and wrestling. The ancient Games had consisted of short races, days-long boxing matches, and chariot races.

Like the ancient Games, organizers held the event every four years, with Paris hosting in 1900, when women made their first appearance. The Paris Games had many more competitors, as 997 athletes represented 24 countries in 95 total events. These Games were spread out from May through October to coincide with the Paris Exposition.

The Summer Olympics have now spanned into the 21st century and have become the ultimate crowning achievement for athletes worldwide. The Games have evolved with the addition and removal of events, the scope of media coverage, the addition of a separate Winter Olympics, and the emergence of both the Special Olympics and Paralympic Games.

The Olympics have been the site of great athletic feats and sportsmanship. They have presented tragedy, triumph, controversy, and political grandstanding. There have been legendary athletes, remarkable human-interest stories, doping allegations, boycotts, terrorist attacks, and three cancellations because of worldwide war.

Yet the Olympics, with its five interlocking rings and eternal flame, remain a symbol of unity and hope.

The United States hosted its first Games in 1904 in St. Louis, Missouri, which, like Paris, spread the Games over several months in conjunction with the World Fair. The presentation of gold, silver, and bronze medals for finishing first, second, and third in each event began at this Olympics.

More than 2,000 athletes competed in England at the 1908 London Games, which were originally scheduled for Rome but reassigned once organizers discovered the Italian capital would not be ready in time. In London, the marathon race was extended by 195 meters so the finish line would be just below the royal box in the stadium and thus the 26.2 miles from the 1908 edition went on to become the official marathon distance beginning with the 1924 Paris Games.

Stockholm, Sweden, hosted the 1912 Games, and the Olympics were cancelled in 1916 because of World War I (WWI). Other years in which the Olympic Games were not held include 1940 and 1944 because of World War II.

Berlin, Germany, had been awarded the 1916 Olympics that were cancelled, but rather than reward the Germans following WWI by giving them the 1920 Games, they were instead awarded to Antwerp, Belgium, to honor the Belgians who suffered so many hardships during the war. The Olympic flag, which shows five interlocked rings to signify the universality of the Games, was first hoisted during the 1920 opening ceremonies in Antwerp. The Olympic rings have become a well-known symbol of sportsmanship and unity worldwide.

The 1924 Games were back in Paris, and the Olympics became a recognized, bona fide worldwide event. The number of participating countries went from 29 to 44. There were more than 3,000 athletes competing and more than 1,000 journalists covering the competition.

Also, in 1924, the annual event became known as the Summer Olympics, or Summer Games, as the Winter Olympics debuted in Chamonix, France. The Winter Games were held every four years through 1992. The Winter Olympics were then held again in 1994 and every four years since then.

Two more long-standing traditions began at the 1928 Summer Games in Amsterdam, Netherlands. The Olympic flame was lit for the first time in a cauldron at the top of the Olympic stadium. Also, during the opening ceremony, the national team of Greece entered the stadium first and the Dutch entered last, signifying the first team to host the modern Olympics and the current host. This tradition still stands today.

The United States got its second Summer Olympics in 1932, when Los Angeles, California, hosted. The city built a lavish coliseum for

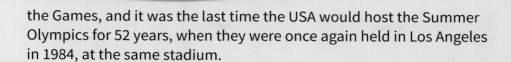

the Games, and it was the last time the USA would host the Summer Olympics for 52 years, when they were once again held in Los Angeles in 1984, at the same stadium.

The 1936 Summer Olympics in Berlin also produced some long-lasting, first-time traditions. These Games were the first to have a torch relay bringing the Olympic flame to the stadium, and they were also the first to be televised.

The Summer Olympics took a 12-year hiatus because of World War II, and London was once again called upon to host the Games with short notice in 1948.

The Summer Games have been held every four years since 1948. In 2016, Rio de Janeiro, Brazil, hosted the Summer Games, and that meant the Olympics had now been held on five continents. Australia has hosted the Summer Olympics twice (Melbourne in 1956 and Sydney in 2000). Asia has hosted four times (Tokyo, Japan in 1964 and 2020; Seoul, Korea, in 1988; and Beijing, China, in 2008).

Other North American cities to host the Summer Olympics have been Mexico City, Mexico, in 1968; Montreal, Canada, in 1976; and Atlanta, Georgia, in 1996 for the centennial anniversary of the modern Olympics. Los Angeles will host the Games for a third time in 2028.

Although athletes typically garner headlines for most Olympic coverage, sometimes events outside of the playing field force the world to take notice.

Eight Palestinian terrorists shot two Israeli athletes dead and held nine more as hostages during the 1972 Munich Games in Germany. Those nine were also murdered during a botched rescue attempt.

The 1980 Moscow Games in Russia saw the fewest number of athletes in a Summer Olympics since 1956, when the USA led a boycott of Moscow after the Soviet Union invaded Afghanistan in December of 1979.

The Soviet Union then led a contingency of Eastern European nations that boycotted the 1984 Los Angeles Games during the Cold War, mainly as payback for the U.S. boycott.

The first Summer Olympics that were boycott-free since 1972 were the 1992 Games in Barcelona, Spain, which was also the first time professional basketball players competed, opening the door for professionals in all Olympic sports except wrestling and boxing. Before the International Olympic Committee (IOC) approved professional athletes to participate in the late 1980s, the Olympics were primarily for the world's best amateur athletes.

Many have lamented the demise of amateurism at the Olympic Games, but by far the most contentious issue the IOC has dealt with in recent years is the scourge of steroids and other prohibited performance-enhancing drugs.

The world's greatest celebration of sport has had a checkered and colorful past, from politics and doping to sheer athleticism and the triumph of the human spirit. This century has seen the Summer Games return to familiar places (Athens 2004, London 2012) and expand to new ones (Sydney 2000, Rio de Janeiro 2016). Tokyo awaits the world in 2020, when the newest great Olympic stories will be told.

– Scott McDonald, Olympic and Paralympic Journalist

ATHLETES TO WATCH IN TOKYO

The 2020 Summer Games in Tokyo will feature several new names making their Olympic debuts, yet many veterans will prolong their impressive careers there as well. They all go to the Olympics looking for the same thing—to stand on the medal podium wearing a gold medal.

Of the hundreds of athletes who will compete in Tokyo, some will be poised to make their marks on the world stage, while others are preparing to build on a legacy forged over multiple Olympic Games.

American swimmers like Caeleb Dressel, Katie Ledecky, and Lilly King will look to shine in the water along with other decorated veterans like Sweden's Sarah Sjöström and Great Britain's Adam Peaty.

Allyson Felix will try to tie Carl Lewis as the most-decorated track and field Olympic athlete in American history. American sprinter Noah Lyles will work to put his first stamp into the Olympic books while other athletes, like World Champion Australian surfer Stephanie Gilmore, could become recognizable names in the five sports making their Olympic debut.

Then there are the Japanese athletes looking to win gold in front of their adoring home crowds, including tennis player Naomi Osaka, who defeated Serena Williams in the 2018 U.S. Open final, and gymnast Takeru Kitazono, who could win up to five medals in the Tokyo Games.

Among all the venues where various events of the 2020 Summer Games will be held—be it the pool, the track, the archery range, or the golf links—Tokyo will be the climax to the 4-year crescendo fueled by World Cups, Pan American Games, and World Championships.

Athletes to Watch introduces you to some new names with great potential and will also remind you of the household name stars destined to be considered among the greatest of Olympians.

SIMONE BILES
USA GYMNASTICS

May Be the Most-Decorated U.S. Olympic Gymnast

Simone Biles began dazzling the gymnastics world long before her Olympic debut at the 2016 Rio de Janeiro Games, where she was almost completely golden. Biles won four gold medals and a bronze in Rio.

Biles' five overall medals at one Olympics equaled an achievement accomplished by only three other American female gymnasts—Mary Lou Retton (1984), Shannon Miller (1992), and Nastia Liukin (2008). In 2016 she also became the only American gymnast other than Gabby Douglas in 2012 to win gold medals in both the individual all-around and the team competitions. At the conclusion of the Rio Games, she became the first American female gymnast to carry the flag during an Olympic closing ceremony.

The 4-foot 8-inch phenom from Houston has been more than just an Olympic standout. Biles won 14 gold, 3 silver, and 3 bronze medals in World Championships from 2013 to 2018. That includes winning the all-around individual title and floor exercise four times each.

After the Rio Games, Biles took the entire 2017 competition season off. She staged a wildly successful comeback in 2018 when she won four gold medals at the World Championships in Doha, Qatar. Her 2019 season revealed stunts in her arsenal that had never been seen—including new jumps and twists in her routine, one good enough to win the 2019 World Cup in Germany and the U.S. Classic in Kentucky.

Biles will be 23 at the 2020 Tokyo Games and, in quite a reversal, the oldest of her gymnastics teammates.

A HERO'S WELCOME

When Simone Biles returned home after her dominance at the 2016 Rio Games, she was greeted at the Houston airport by nearly a thousand fans at a jam-packed terminal. Local dignitaries made remarks, a nearby high school band played, children held signs greeting their hometown hero, and throngs of people gathered to get a glimpse of her and hear her remarks.

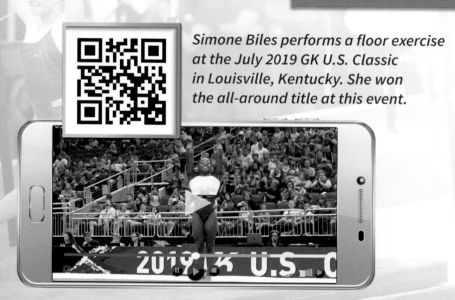

Simone Biles performs a floor exercise at the July 2019 GK U.S. Classic in Louisville, Kentucky. She won the all-around title at this event.

SEBASTIAN BRENDEL
GERMANY CANOEING

Defending Olympic and World Champion in C-1

Sebastian Brendel grew up in Schwedt, Germany, where he first learned canoeing at the age of eight. He moved to Potsdam so that he could attend school for aspiring athletes, and apart from canoeing, he also dabbled in other sports.

Brendel played soccer, ran track, and practiced karate, but he eventually ditched them all when he gravitated to canoe sprinting as a sport. He made his international debut in 2007, which is the same time that American swimmer Michael Phelps was becoming an international star. Brendel said Phelps was one of his most-admired heroes.

Brendel eventually made a big splash on the canoe sprinting scene. At the 2012 London Games, he won gold in the C-1 1,000 meters. At the 2016 Rio de Janeiro Games, he won gold in both the C-1 1,000 meters and C-2 1,000 meters with teammate Jan Vandrey.

Brendel broke the world record in the C-1 1,000 meters at the 2014 International Canoe Federation Sprint World Championships in Moscow, Russia. He has six World Cup titles and has been named regional and national athlete of the year multiple times in Germany.

S. BRENDEL

GER

Brendel also has 10 European titles and four second-place finishes in races from the C-4 200 meters to relays to the C-1 5,000 meters. The rangy 6-foot 4-inch canoe sprinter still competes with the KC Potsdam Club.

Brendel, who will be 32 at the time of the 2020 Tokyo Games, is still going strong and should once again be a favorite to reach the medal podium while defending both of his Olympic titles.

A NATIONAL SPORTS HERO

Germany confers awards on athletes for national and international sports accomplishments, and Brendel is no stranger to accepting those honors. After the 2012 London Games, he was awarded the Silbernen Lorbeerblatt (Silver Laurel Leaf), which is the highest honor bestowed on athletes by the national government. In 2015, he was named Champion of the Year.

Here is a video showing Sebastian Brendel's technique in both training and competition. The German is the two-time defending Olympic champion in the C1 1,000 meters.

JORDAN BURROUGHS
USA WRESTLING

Could Be Most-Decorated U.S. Olympic Wrestler

Jordan Burroughs began wrestling at age five, about the same time when elementary kids begin tussling on the playground at school. He took up the sport after watching his television heroes Ultimate Warrior and "Macho Man" Randy Savage, who were entertainment wrestlers.

Burroughs became a state champion as a high school wrestler in New Jersey before going west to wrestle at the University of Nebraska, where he won two national titles. In college, he was awarded the Dan Hodge Trophy, which is given to the nation's top collegiate wrestler.

Burroughs entered the freestyle wrestling arena after college and immediately started winning. He qualified for the 2012 London Games and eventually defeated Iran's Sadegh Goudarzi to win an Olympic gold medal.

Prior to London, Burroughs had won the 2011 World Championship, a feat he accomplished again in 2013. Burroughs went on to win 69 consecutive matches, which set an American record, before he was denied another world title in 2014. He finished third at the 2014 World Championships but came back to win the world title in 2015.

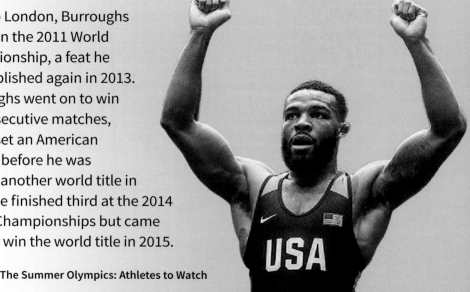

SLOW STARTER

After a stellar high school career in New Jersey, Jordan Burroughs wrestled at the University of Nebraska. In his freshman season, Burroughs had an average record of just 16 wins and 13 losses. After a national level third-place finish in a much-improved sophomore year, he went undefeated in his last 2 years, winning two national championships.

The 2016 Rio de Janeiro Games turned out to be disappointing as Burroughs, then ranked number one in the world, lost twice and did not medal. However, he did bounce back to win the 2017 World Championship.

Burroughs now needs two more international gold medals—between Olympics and World Championships—to surpass the six-time champion John Smith and become the most-decorated American wrestler of all time.

MIXED MARTIAL ARTS FOR BURROUGHS?

Burroughs had so much success during his early years on the international scene that he was often asked if he would consider competing in mixed martial arts. But Burroughs, a true wrestler, resisted the allure of big money pro fights, stuck to his roots, and kept his focus on winning wrestling championships.

ELI DERSHWITZ
USA FENCING

Youngest American Saber Champion Seeks Gold

Eli Dershwitz stormed on to the saber fencing scene early in his youth and has been a rising star for the United States ever since.

Growing up in Massachusetts, Dershwitz followed the footsteps of his brother, Phil, who was also a fencer. Eli was skillful at a young age. He became the country's top-ranked fencer on the junior circuit in 2013 at just 17, and 1 year later he became the youngest saber fencer on the senior circuit to win a U.S. title.

Dershwitz kept training and moving up the world ranks. In 2015, he won the Under-20 World Championships, making him a five-time junior world champion. Dershwitz made the U.S. Olympic Team for the 2016 Rio de Janeiro Games, where he lost in Round 16.

Dershwitz accomplished all of this before his sophomore year at Harvard University, where he also competed. He won a pair of NCAA titles at Harvard and was named all-American at his sport. Dershwitz was the first-ever male fencer at the Ivy League University to win consecutive fencing titles.

Competing at the 2017 Maccabiah Games in Israel, Dershwitz won two gold medals.

YOUNG PRODIGY

Dershwitz gained recognition as a fierce fencer late in high school and early in his time at Harvard. By the summer of 2016—between his freshman and sophomore years—he was the top-ranked American saber fencer and among the top 10 in the world. By July 2018, Dershwitz was top ranked in the world. He will be just 24 when the 2020 Tokyo Games begin.

He defeated his Harvard teammate Philippe Guy for gold in the individual event and then won gold in the team event with Guy, Ben Stone, and Matt Rothenberg as they defeated Israel in the finals.

Now a Harvard graduate with a degree in History, Dershwitz heads to Tokyo in 2020 where he could become the youngest American to win an Olympic gold medal in men's saber.

INTERNATIONAL EXPERIENCE

Dershwitz has competed on the international scene for several years, including five World Championships and one Olympic Games. Although his 19th-place finish at the 2016 Rio de Janeiro Games was a slight disappointment, he has flourished in other competitions, including winning a silver medal at the 2018 World Championships in Wuxi, China.

DING/LIU RIVALRY
CHINA TABLE TENNIS

Will the Teammates Battle for Gold?

Liu Shiwen and Ding Ning are two of the best table tennis players ever to pick up a paddle. Between them, the women have won four of the five World Championships in women's singles table tennis from 2011 to 2019. Ding had already won Olympic medals in the sport, winning silver at London 2012 and gold at Rio 2016. Liu, who was a reserve on the London team, missed out on the Rio Games due to a controversial decision by the Chinese federation.

In early 2016, Liu was the top-ranked player in the world and was a favorite to challenge for the gold medal. She was cruising toward securing a spot on the Olympic team when she suffered a shocking upset at the hands of 19-year-old Doo Hoi-kem from Hong Kong. This loss caused Chinese team officials to pick Ding instead. The other women's spot on the team went to defending gold medalist Li Xiaoxia.

Ding went on to win the gold without having to beat Liu. At the World Championships, since 2011 the two have each made it through to either the finals or semifinals. They have played each other three times, with Ding winning in the semifinals in 2013 and the final in 2015. Liu beat Ding in 2019

Liu Shiwen

Ding Ning

on the way to winning the title. In 2017, Liu lost her semifinal, failing to advance to face Ding, who defended her title. The two did pair up to win doubles gold that year.

The two great champions and teammates will be the class of the field in Tokyo, providing a big advantage for China and a big treat for fans.

AVOWED RIVALS

Liu and Ding are teammates, and at times even doubles partners. One thing they are not, however, is friends. The seeds of their rivalry were sowed leading up to both the 2012 and 2016 Games. Ding was given a featured role at each while Liu was relegated to reserve or team duties despite her top ranking. In 2020, Liu and her rival are destined to clash again.

"We have played together since a very young age, seeing each other in practice every day, but also competing against each other on the court. In fact, we spend more time together than with our family members. But because of this long-time rivalry, our relationship seems to be close but is also quite distant."

— Liu Shiwen

CAELEB DRESSEL
USA SWIMMING

Chance to Match Michael Phelps

Caeleb Dressel is one of the top American swimmers heading into the 2020 Tokyo Games, which makes him one of the faces most likely to be seen during these Olympics.

Dressel is a Florida native who has been a college national champion, a U.S. national champion, an Olympic champion, and most recently, a world champion.

The freestyle sprinter won multiple NCAA titles at the University of Florida and won two gold medals at the 2016 Rio de Janeiro Games in the 4x100-meter freestyle relay and 4x100-meter medley relay.

Since the 2016 Games, Dressel has become a household name in swimming, winning seven individual and 13 total World Championship gold medals.

At the 2017 World Championships in Hungary, Dressel won seven gold medals in these events:

- 50-meter freestyle
- 100-meter freestyle
- 100-meter butterfly
- 4x100-meter freestyle relay
- 4x100-meter medley relay
- 4x100-meter mixed freestyle relay
- 4x100-meter mixed medley relay

Dressel is only the second swimmer to win seven gold medals at a World Championships.

Michael Phelps accomplished the same feat in 2007—a year before winning an Olympic record eight gold medals at the 2008 Beijing Games.

At the 2019 World Championships, Dressel broke Phelps' 10-year-old world record in the 100-meter butterfly. He won three other individual gold medals, defending his 2017 titles and adding the 50-meter butterfly. He should threaten to medal in up to seven events (relay events included) at the 2020 Games.

SPRINT PROWESS

Caeleb Dressel has been a bona fide sprinter ever since his days growing up in Florida through his collegiate time at the University of Florida. He has won championships in freestyle and butterfly, both in short course (yards) and long course (meters). With the Olympics adding more sprint events, Dressel will be an even greater medal threat in Tokyo.

Check out this compilation summarizing Dressel's sizzling 2017 World Championships performances.

BRADY ELLISON
USA ARCHERY

Recent World Champion Seeks First Olympic Gold

Brady Ellison began shooting arrows while hunting with his family in Arizona. He got so proficient that he turned into a world-class archer. Now, he competes on the Olympic team against a younger generation who learned the skill after watching *The Hunger Games*.

Regardless of how they learned or how they got there, Ellison is still the benchmark for American archery, and he is one of the favorites heading to the 2020 Tokyo Games.

Often called the "Arizona Cowboy," Ellison was America's top recurve archer from 2007 to 2019. After winning the 2019 World Championship, Ellison is considered a favorite to win gold in Tokyo—in perhaps both the individual and team events.

Despite winning team silver at the 2012 London Games, Ellison left Europe disappointed. He felt his individual performance could have been better.

"In London I just shot bad and got beat. It was a wonderful venue," Ellison told Team USA. "My best chance of medaling individually was probably in Beijing."

WHAT SLUMP?

After a disappointing individual finish at the 2012 London Games and slight drop in the world rankings in 2013, people in the archery world thought Ellison might be in a slump. The Arizona native shrugged off those notions and kept himself in the world's top 10 rankings, winning two medals at the 2016 Rio de Janeiro Games and the 2019 World Championship.

Ellison did not medal at the 2008 Beijing Games, but he won two medals in the 2016 Rio de Janeiro, team silver and an individual bronze. The American team looked poised to wrap up a gold medal; however, the South Koreans were perfect in their final round, securing the title.

Ellison is refocused now, as shown by winning his first world outdoor championship in 2019 in the Netherlands, something he called "bigger than winning bronze at the Games."

WORLD CUP DOMINANCE

Brady Ellison has been the top American recurve archer for more than a decade, and he's won the World Cup multiple times. He won individual gold medals in 2010 (Edinburgh), 2011 (Istanbul), 2014 (Lausanne), and 2016 (Odense). He also won silver in 2017 and bronze in both 2013 and 2018.

ALLYSON FELIX
USA TRACK AND FIELD

Chance to Tie the All-Time Medal Count in Track

Allyson Felix follows a long line of track athletes from Southern California who ran their way into Olympic lore. Already a decorated Olympian, she has the potential to break one of the greatest records in American track history.

Felix has nine Olympic medals—six gold and three silver—which is two shy of Carl Lewis' career mark of 11, the most by any American male or female in track. Should she win three more medals, she would stand above any American in Olympic track and field history.

Felix hit the international scene at just age 18 by winning the 200 meters silver medal at the 2004 Athens Games. At the 2008 Beijing Games, she replicated her silver in the 200 meters—her strongest event. She also won her first gold medal in a relay at Beijing.

Things began to turn gold for Felix individually at the 2012 London Games, when she finally won the 200 meters and also the 4x100-meter relay and 4x400-meter relay gold medals, thus becoming the first American woman to win three gold medals in a single Olympic track meet since Florence Griffith-Joyner in 1988.

Felix won two more relay gold medals along with a silver medal in the 400 meters at the 2016 Rio Games, giving her a career total of six Olympic gold medals and three silver medals. She also has 11 total World Championship gold medals.

Felix took a break from training in 2018 to have a baby before coming back for the 2019 season at age 33. For her, a three-medal haul in Tokyo would be quite a feat.

BABY'S BATTLE

Felix's daughter Camryn was born in November 2018, 8 weeks before she was due. An emergency C-section was needed, and the baby girl was in the neonatal intensive care unit for weeks. Despite this harrowing experience, once Camryn was healthy, it was back to training for Felix, who was back on the track competing just 8 months after giving birth.

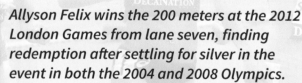

Allyson Felix wins the 200 meters at the 2012 London Games from lane seven, finding redemption after settling for silver in the event in both the 2004 and 2008 Olympics.

JANJA GARNBRET
SLOVENIA SPORT CLIMBING

World's Top-Ranked Climber Headlines New Sport

Sport climbing will make its Olympic debut at the 2020 Games in Tokyo, giving the world a chance to watch 20-year-old sensation Janja Garnbret of Slovenia in action.

Her ascension in the sport has been remarkably fast and impressive, as Garnbret is the world's top-ranked female climber in lead and bouldering, which are two of the three disciplines that comprise sport climbing (speed climbing is the third).

Garnbret fell in love with climbing at an early age and by the time she hit her teens she was dominating the youth sport climbing circuit, winning five World Championships.

In 2015, when she was eligible for the International Federation of Sport Climbing (IFSC) World Cup, Garnbret was thrilled to be able to shift her focus to tangling with the best in the world—and her winning ways continued.

At the IFSC World Championships at Innsbruck, Austria, in 2018, she topped a field oozing with talent by snatching gold in bouldering and combined, along with a silver medal in lead. With that victory, Garnbret became the first female climber to claim world titles in both lead and bouldering.

Going into the 2019 season, Garnbret already had 19 World Cup wins on her résumé to go with three World Championships. She swept the season's six bouldering events, which had never been done before.

Possessing an insatiable appetite for improvement, the history-making champion is now ready to add to her already impressive list of achievements at the Tokyo Games.

VICTORY IN VAIL

In early June, the 2019 bouldering season came to a close at the annual Mountain Games in Vail, Colorado, where Janja Garnbret dominated, as usual, and was crowned the overall bouldering World Cup season champion. In bouldering, ropes and harnesses aren't used, but climbers typically compete at heights of about 20 feet.

To watch Janja Garnbret compete in bouldering at the 2019 IFSC World Cup in Vail, Colorado, scan here.

STEPHANIE GILMORE
AUSTRALIA SURFING

Seven-Time World Champion

Surfing will make its Olympic debut at the 2020 Tokyo Games, and if there is one athlete who is sure to be a favorite, it is Stephanie Gilmore.

Australian Stephanie Gilmore, who goes by the nickname "Happy Gilmore," is one of the most-decorated female surfers in the world. She has won seven world titles and should be the headliner as the Tokyo Games take on a new wave of events.

A native of New South Wales, Gilmore began surfing at the age of 10 when she first hopped up on a body board and began riding the waves.

While a teenager, Gilmore won wild card events in her country during 2005 and 2006 before becoming a hit on the international circuit as a 19-year-old in 2007, winning the Association of Surfing Professionals World Title at Honolua Bay, Hawaii. She did not stop there, though, winning more world titles in 2008, 2009, 2010, 2012, and 2014. Gilmore also won the World Surf League (name change from ASP in 2015) in 2018 at Jeffreys Bay, South Africa, giving her seven total world titles.

In addition to her prowess at winning the WSL World Title Race, Gilmore has

OLYMPIC TEST RUN

Since surfing is making its first Olympic appearance in 2020, a test event was held in 2019. The "Ready Steady Tokyo" event held a year in advance examined things such as weather, surf break, and wave size. Logistically, things such as technology, event format, live scoring, presentation, and security were evaluated to help surfing make a great Olympic debut.

typically been a force on the ASP/WSL Championship Tour—with the exception of 2015 when she was mostly injured and did not compete. Almost half of her Tour wins have come off the shores of her native Australia.

The Tokyo Games will present an unprecedented stage in the sport of surfing. Although Gilmore will be 32 years old when the 2020 Tokyo Games begin, she is still the one to watch.

WORLD VISION

In Australia, Gilmore lives a laid-back, surfer lifestyle. As a philanthropist, however, she works diligently with the Coeur de Forêt foundation, which builds and equips water wells in the African nation of Senegal. She has been a long-time supporter of World Vision as a children's sponsor in Kenya and Ethiopia.

JASON KENNY
GREAT BRITAIN CYCLING

Could Become the Most-Decorated British Olympian

Jason Kenny has just about done it all on a bicycle. He began competing on the Union Cycliste Internationale (UCI) Track Cycling World Cup circuit in 2006. He has since won multiple World Cup races in individual and team events. He has even won keirin-style races, in which a motorcycle paces the cyclists.

Kenny could have ridden into the sunset after the 2016 Rio de Janeiro Games in Brazil. He had just won three gold medals, bringing his career Olympic medal count to seven—six of them gold.

Kenny won his third team gold in Rio after winning the team event at the 2008 Beijing Games and again at the 2012 London Games. In front of his compatriots in London, he set a new Olympic record in individual qualifying when he clocked 10.38 seconds for a 200-meter final lap.

Kenny has won three individual gold medals and one silver medal. His six Olympic gold medals are equal to the most of any British athlete.

Sweeping gold in his three events in Rio made him consider calling it quits.

"Slowly but surely I'd just had enough," Kenny said in *Cyclist*

magazine. "I'd been doing it for so long. I didn't realize at the time, but I'd never really taken a break. In over a decade at the most I'd had a couple of weeks off, and even then, I was still thinking about training."

A year away from the bike let Kenny's body recuperate. And when he did get back on it, he felt invigorated and ready to keep moving forward and make yet another Olympic team.

AN ACCIDENTAL RETURN

Kenny did not officially retire from the sport after winning three sprint cycling gold medals in Rio, but he did take a substantial amount of time off. The fire to compete came back while he was filming a project in a velodrome. He felt reenergized and decided it was time to get back on the track and start training for Tokyo 2020.

British track cyclist Jason Kenny rides to a new Olympic record at the 2012 London Games before a raucous home crowd.

LILLY KING
USA SWIMMING

Two-Time Olympic Gold Medalist

Within the space of a few months in 2016, Indiana native Lilly King won NCAA titles and Olympic medals, shattered records, and turned a lot of heads as one of the new and very talented faces of USA swimming.

During her freshman year at Indiana University, King won the 100- and 200-yard breaststroke at the NCAA Finals on her way to being named both the Big Ten Freshman of the Year and Big Ten Swimmer of the Year, along with earning All-American accolades.

King went to the 2016 Rio de Janeiro Games riding a wave of confidence, and in the 100-meter breaststroke final the 19-year-old outdueled Russia's Yuliya Efimova, the reigning world champion, to win the gold medal and set an Olympic record time of 1:04.93. King also swam the breaststroke leg on Team USA's gold medal-winning 4x100-meter medley relay team.

King then became a dominating presence at the World Championships. In 2017, she set world records in Budapest, Hungary, by winning both the 50-meter breaststroke (29.40) and 100-meter breaststroke (1:04.13).

CHANGING LANES

During King's high school swimming days in Evansville, Indiana, her school team shared a pool with five other teams, often making practices congested and challenging to navigate with so many bodies in the water. She added morning practices several times a week with local swim teams to supplement her workouts—and to enjoy having a lane to herself to swim in.

At the 2019 World Championships in Gwangju, South Korea, King won the 50-meter breaststroke, becoming just the second swimmer to win consecutive world titles in that event. She was also the first to the wall in the 100-meter breaststroke, where she edged teammate Katie Meili and Efimova.

King is poised and ready for more gold medals at the 2020 Tokyo Games, where the dual world record holder will look to continue her winning ways.

RUSSIAN RIVAL

Plenty of drama surrounded King's races with Russia's Efimova during the 2016 Games. The International Olympic Committee attempted to prevent Efimova from competing due to her having repeatedly failed drug tests for banned substances. King was vocal in her belief that Efimova should have been banned, and the two have continued exchanging words ever since.

TAKERU KITAZONO
JAPAN GYMNASTICS

Five Gold Medals at 2018 Youth Olympic Games

Japanese teen gymnastics sensation Takeru Kitazono put a stranglehold on the spotlight at the 2018 Youth Olympic Games, thanks to an epic performance never before produced at this level.

Kitazono, just 15 years old at the time of those Games in Buenos Aires, Argentina, won gold in each of the all-around, floor exercise, rings, parallel bars, and horizontal bar events, becoming the first gymnast to ever haul home five gold medals from a single Youth Olympic Games.

This performance for the ages also made Kitazono the first Japanese athlete to win five individual gold medals at any International Olympic Committee (IOC)-sanctioned Games. You have to go all the way back to 1992 to find a gymnast who had achieved this feat—Vitaly Scherbo at the Summer Games in Barcelona, Spain. The lone event where Kitazono failed to medal was the pommel horse, where he wound up sixth. He also helped Japan win the team silver medal.

Kitazono began 2019 by helping Japan win an international meet in Houston, taking first place on the parallel bars, the rings, and on his nemesis in Buenos Aires, the pommel horse.

In June 2019, Kitazono and his Japanese teammates claimed the first gold medal of the inaugural Artistic Gymnastics Junior World Championships in Hungary.

Kitazono has been a dominant performer in junior meets and is now ready to take the next step and compete against the best in the world in his home country when it hosts the 2020 Summer Games.

KOHEI NUMBER TWO

Kitazono's rise in the sport has earned him the nickname "Kohei Number Two." That is in reference to Kohei Uchimura, the legendary Japanese gymnast who is a three-time Olympic gold medalist and six-time world all-around champion. Uchimura won the all-around title at the 2012 and 2016 Olympics and is regarded as one of the greatest gymnasts of all time.

To watch Takeru Kitazono's gold medal routine on the horizontal bar at the 2018 Youth Olympic Games, scan here.

BROOKS KOEPKA
USA GOLF

Four-Time Major Champion

Over the past two years, Brooks Koepka has played some of the best golf ever seen.

Bombing 300-plus yard drives, striking flag-seeking iron shots, and rolling in clutch putts when he needs them, he has cracked golf's history books with his must-see style of play.

Koepka's charge to greatness began in 2017 at the U.S. Open. Despite having just a single Professional Golfer's Association win to his credit, he shot three rounds in the 60s to win at Erin Hills in Wisconsin. A year later, at revered Shinnecock Hills in New York, he shot a final-round 68 to win by a stroke and become the first man in 29 years to win back-to-back U.S. Open titles.

Two months later Koepka held off Tiger Woods to win his third major, the PGA Championship at Bellerive Country Club in St. Louis. Then, in 2019, he won the PGA title for the second straight time in grand fashion, as he led after every round at New York's Bethpage Black, marking just the fifth time that had ever been done in the history of the tournament.

With that win Koepka also became the first golfer in history to hold consecutive titles at two different major championships

RED, WHITE, AND BLUE

Koepka has teed it up in international competition for the USA on several occasions. He contributed three points in the Americans' 2016 Ryder Cup victory at Hazeltine National Golf Club in Minnesota, and he won two matches and lost two for the USA in its Presidents Cup win in 2017. He was part of the 2018 U.S. Ryder Cup team that lost to Europe.

simultaneously. He finished in the top four of every major in 2019.

Koepka also became a member of the exclusive group of golfers who have won four majors in less than two years: Ben Hogan, Arnold Palmer, Jack Nicklaus, and Tiger Woods.

Koepka, the 2018 PGA Player of the Year, is a strong contender to win every time he tees it up.

EXCELLENT IN EUROPE

Koepka got his professional start in Europe, where he quickly showcased his skills and earned the European Tour's Sir Henry Cotton Rookie of the Year award in 2014. The award is named after Sir Henry Cotton, who was a three-time winner of the Open Championship. Fellow four-time major winner Rory McIlroy won the tour's Player of the Year award that season.

KLIMENT KOLESNIKOV
RUSSIA SWIMMING

Teen Holds 10 World Junior Records

In July 2019, Kliment Kolesnikov, a 19-year-old Russian swimmer, won a bronze medal in the 50-meter backstroke at the World Championships in South Korea.

Although it was Kolesnikov's first senior individual World Championship medal, the result was a little disappointing considering the teen is the world record holder in the event. Given the spectacular junior career he enjoyed, he'll likely be having shinier medals draped around his neck for many years to come.

Kolesnikov barged onto the international swimming scene at the 2016 European Junior Championships, where he won both the 50- and 100-meter backstrokes, setting world junior records in the process.

Kolesnikov earned a spot in the 200-meter backstroke at the 2017 World Championships in Budapest, Hungary, after he broke the world junior record in that event at the Russian Championships. At the age of 17, he swam a solid race, missing out on a bronze medal by 0.08 seconds. He did lower his world junior record to 1:55.15.

Kolesnikov's 2018 season was filled with dazzling performances and times worthy of competing on the world stage. At the European Championships in Glasgow, Scotland, he swept both the 50- and 100-meter backstroke titles, setting new world junior records in both the events. In the 50-meter race he also broke the nine-year-old senior world record.

Tokyo 2020 may well be Kolesnikov's coming out party, but if not, it is hard to imagine that it will be much farther away.

SILVER DOE

In 2019, Kolesnikov was presented with a Silver Doe award at the Russian Olympic Committee headquarters in Moscow. The annual ceremony is held by the Russian Federation of Sports Journalists for Russian athletes and coaches who have distinguished themselves in their respective sports that year. There are typically 10 recipients each year.

To watch Kliment Kolesnikov win the 100-meter backstroke at the Russian Championships in 2018, scan here.

MARIYA LASITSKENE
RUSSIA TRACK AND FIELD

Seeking Elusive Olympic Gold

Mariya Lasitskene has zapped a lot of suspense from the women's high jump these days, thanks to an extraordinary string of dominating performances across the globe.

The lanky 5-foot 11- inch Russian won the World Indoor Championships in Poland in 2014, and then won the World Championships the next year. Ten months later, Lasitskene won a meet in Smolensk, Russia, which marked the beginning of a mind-boggling 45-meet winning streak that lasted more than 2 years, and this was followed by her second World Championship in London, England, in 2017.

If you are thinking that Lasitskene must then have won an Olympic gold medal, that would make sense. She could have won one, but she did not get the chance. Her 45-meet winning streak did not include the 2016 Rio Olympics. This is because the IOC banned the entire Russian track and field team from competing in the Rio because of multiple doping violations. She was later cleared to compete as a neutral athlete, but not until several months after the

Games. The winning height in Rio was 1.97 meters (6.46 feet). Lasitskene regularly cleared 2 meters (6.56 feet) to win meets, and she has even cleared 2.06 meters (6.76 feet).

With multiple indoor and outdoor World Championship medals in her trophy case, all Lasitskene wants is a shot at that Olympic gold. She rarely surrenders that top spot on the podium and will look to continue her domination in her first Summer Olympics at Tokyo 2020.

NAVIGATING IN NEUTRAL

Since April 2017, Lasitskene has competed as an Authorized Neutral Athlete. This is the designation for Russian athletes cleared to compete at international track and field events since their country's federation was banned for systematic doping. Russia has been stripped of 43 Olympic medals due to doping, by far the most of any country.

To watch Mariya Lasitskene clear 2.04 meters *(6.69 feet)* to win the women's high jump at the 2018 IAAF Diamond League meet in Paris, scan here.

KATIE LEDECKY
USA SWIMMING

Five-Time Olympic Gold Medalist Building Legacy

Katie Ledecky burst into the swimming scene at age 15, and she has been breaking the record books and piling up the medals ever since.

As the youngest swimmer at the 2012 U.S. Olympic Trials, all Ledecky did was win the 800-meter freestyle and finish third in the 400-meter freestyle.

When the 2012 Summer Games in London rolled around, the 15-year-old Ledecky was unfazed by the pressure-packed surroundings as she swam to gold in the 800-meter freestyle while bettering Janet Evans' long-standing American record by more than a second.

Four years later at the 2016 Rio Olympics, Ledecky turned in an epic performance by scooping up five medals, four of them gold. She became just the second woman, after Debbie Meyer in 1968, to sweep the 200-, 400-, and 800-meter freestyles at an Olympics.

Ledecky lowered her own world records in both the 400 and 800 meters and won the latter by a stunning 11 seconds over her nearest competitor. In a tightly contested 200, she held off Sweden's Sarah Sjöström for gold, and she anchored Team USA's victorious 4x200-meter freestyle relay.

In total, Ledecky has broken the world record in the 400 meters (three times)

DOMINANT DEBUT

In the first race of Katie Ledecky's professional career, at a Pro Swim Series meet in Indianapolis in 2018, she chopped a whopping 5 seconds off her world record time in winning the 1500-meter freestyle. As she plowed through the water, her performance was so dominant that she finished almost 50 seconds ahead of the second-place finisher in the race.

the 800 meters (five times), and the 1,500 meters (six times).

While the 2019 World Championships didn't go as Ledecky had hoped—she won just one gold in the 800-meter freestyle and had to pull out of some races due to sickness—she will still be a strong contender for gold in several events at the 2020 Games.

SHIP SPONSOR

Ledecky's legendary career earned her a special award in 2016 when she was chosen, along with Olympic gymnastics great Simone Biles, as sponsor of the USS Enterprise, a Navy aircraft carrier. A ship sponsor is a tradition in which a female civilian is invited to sponsor a ship to bring it good luck and protection for all those who travel on it.

NOAH LYLES
USA TRACK AND FIELD

Possible Three Gold Medals at 2020 Games

Noah Lyles has big dreams for the 2020 Tokyo Games, and leading up to them he showed why those aspirations could be turned into a golden reality.

At the 2019 Outdoor Track and Field Championships in Des Moines, Iowa, the Florida native settled into the starting blocks for the 200-meter finals—his best event—and reeled off a 19.78 seconds time in rainy conditions on his way to victory.

The 22-year-old Lyles has already run both the 100 and 200 meters faster than world record holder Usain Bolt did at the same age.

Also, in 2019 Lyles ran a personal best 19.50 in the 200 meters at a Diamond League meet in Lausanne, Switzerland. It was the eighth-fastest time ever and placed his name alongside this elite trifecta of talent— Michael Johnson, Yohan Blake, and Usain Bolt—as the only other men to have run the event faster.

Lyles also set a personal best in the 100 meters in 2019, running a 9.86 at a meet in China.

Lyles showed flashes of greatness early in his career, winning a gold medal in the 200 meters at the 2014 Youth Olympic Games in China, and grabbing gold in the

FROM THE TUMBLING MAT TO THE TRACK

Lyles spent much of his youth in Gainesville, Florida, and then Alexandria, Virginia, participating in gymnastics and basketball. When he got around to trying track and field at the age of 12, he started with the high jump. Eventually, he tried some running events and quickly found out what the rest of the world is now fully aware of—he is really fast.

100 meters and 4x100-meter relay at the 2016 World Under-20 Championships in Poland.

In 2017, Lyles set the world record for 300 meters indoors, and in 2018 he won the 100 meters at the U.S. Championships.

Noah Lyles wants to win three gold medals at the 2020 Summer Olympics—in the 100-, 200- and 4x100-meter relay—and he has shown the speed required to pull off such a feat.

FLASH OF GREATNESS

Lyles didn't make the U.S. team at the 2016 Olympic Trials, but he sure did make quite an impression. After winning his semifinal heat in the 200 meters, he came back and finished fourth in the finals in a field that oozed world-class talents. His time of 20.09 seconds broke a national high school record that stood for more than three decades.

KEVIN MAYER
FRANCE TRACK AND FIELD

Decathlon World Record Holder

There was a time when the Olympic decathlon champion was considered to be the best athlete in the world. Today, that list is crowded with high-profile professional athletes from international soccer and the major North American sports. Any of these would be hard-pressed to compete head-to-head with Kevin Mayer.

Mayer holds the world record in the decathlon, which is a combination of 10 different track and field events in which points are assigned based on the result of each event. The athlete with the most points after these 10 events is the winner:

- 100 meters
- 400 meters
- 110-meter hurdles
- 1,500 meters
- Long jump
- Shot put
- High jump
- Discus
- Pole Vault
- Javelin

Mayer made a name for himself at the 2014 World Championships, when he topped 8,500 points for the first time to win a silver medal. At the 2016 Rio Games. The Frenchman set his country's national record by breaking 8,800 points for the first time.

WORLD'S GREATEST ATHLETE

This unofficial title was first bestowed upon Jim Thorpe, who won the decathlon at the 1912 Olympics in Stockholm, Sweden. King Gustaf V of Sweden presented medals to the top three finishers. When he came to Thorpe, he told the 25-year-old Native American that he was "the greatest athlete in the world," a title that stuck for decades to follow.

As expected, however, the gold went to then-world record holder and two-time Olympic champion, American Ashton Eaton, who scored 8,893 points.

Mayer was just 24 years old in Rio, but he continued to improve. Always strong in the field events, he steadily got better on the track. In 2017, he won his first World Championship. Then in 2018, at a meet in France, Mayer set personal bests in five events to score a record 9,126 and become only the third man ever to break 9,000 points. In Tokyo, the gold will be his to lose.

"I've been waiting for this moment for a long time. We live for moments like this that are simply incredible. I couldn't cry. I don't have any more tears left because I was crying so much before the 1500 m."

— Kevin Mayer

SYDNEY MCLAUGHLIN
USA TRACK AND FIELD

2016 Olympian Hurdler Ready to Go for Gold

When Sydney McLaughlin qualified for the 2016 U.S. Olympic Team in the 400-meter hurdles as a 16-year-old, there was little question where her career was headed.

Competing at the U.S. Track and Field Trials against a stacked field, McLaughlin ran 54.15 to break the world junior record that had stood since 1984 and grabbed third place to punch her ticket to Rio.

When McLaughlin took the track in Rio a week after celebrating her 17th birthday, she became the youngest American track athlete to compete in an Olympics since 1972.

Following a glorious prep career, McLaughlin spent a year at the University of Kentucky before turning pro, and she made the most of her stay in Lexington. She won the 400-meter hurdles at the Southeastern Conference (SEC) Outdoor Track and Field Championships with an NCAA-record time of 52.75. That was the 13th fastest time ever recorded, and it lowered McLaughlin's own junior world record. She went on to win the NCAA as well.

McLaughlin's indoor season was just as sensational. She won the SEC indoor 400-meter title and took second in the quarter mile at the NCAA Championships with a time of 50.36, the second-fastest collegiate indoor time ever run.

RECORD-SETTING PREP

McLaughlin enjoyed a record-filled prep career at Union Catholic Regional High School in Scotch Plains, NJ, where she didn't lose a race over her final 3 years. She was the Gatorade National High School Athlete of the Year in 2016 and 2017 and set the New Jersey state record with 11 individual career gold medals at the Meet of Champions.

In 2019, the rising 19-year-old star made a smashing Diamond League debut, winning the 400-meter hurdles by overtaking 2016 Olympic champion and U.S. teammate Dalilah Muhammad on the final hurdle.

Sydney McLaughlin has arrived and it's no surprise it was a fast trip.

FAST FEET IN THE FAMILY

McLaughlin grew up in an athletic family that found success on the track. Her father was a semi-finalist in the 400 meters at the 1984 Olympic Trials. Her older brother Taylor brought home a silver medal in the 400-meter hurdles at the IAAF World Under-20 Championships in 2016. Her mom was a runner in high school, as was her older sister Morgan.

KENTO MOMOTA
JAPAN BADMINTON

Number One Player Seeking Redemption After Being Banned

The year 2016 was not a good one for Kento Momota. It started well enough for the then 21-year-old, as he had rocketed to second in the world rankings of men's singles badminton players. The Rio Olympics were approaching and Momota was poised to challenge for a medal. All that changed in the spring of 2016.

Momota and teammate Kenichi Tago were caught gambling at an illegal casino. Gambling is not against the rules of the Badminton World Federation, but because it is illegal in Japan, the country's Nippon Badminton Association (NPA) banned the players. Momota was banned from competing for one year and therefore missed the 2016 Rio Olympic Games.

Disgraced, Momota spent the year reflecting on his mistake and came back determined to prove himself. He was reinstated in May 2017, and from there Momota steadily regained his once-world class form. He did not win an event until the Badminton Asia championships in April 2018 where he stunned everyone by easily defeating third seed and defending Olympic champion

ADVANCE SWEEP

At the 2019 Japanese Open, badminton fans in Tokyo got what they hoped was a preview of the competition at the 2020 Tokyo Games. Momota won the men's singles event, while the women's title went to his countrywoman Akane Yamaguchi. It was the first home team sweep of the event, and a sign that the home court advantage might go a long way at the 2020 Games.

Chen Long of China in the final. The win moved Momota up to number 12 in the world rankings. By late September, the comeback was complete, as Momota reached the number one spot.

Momota is likely to go into Tokyo as the favorite for gold in 2020. These will be his home Olympics in a venue he has won at many times. The pressure to win in front of his countrymen and women will be immense. This time, Momota will need to bet on himself.

STARTING OVER

Momota was with teammate Kenichi Tago when he went to play the illegal baccarat tables in Japan. Momota sat out for a year and came back better than ever. Tago was not so lucky. The NPA banned him in Japan forever. Formerly the third-ranked player in the world, Tago ended up in Malaysia, playing in a competitive league and coaching the women's national team.

NAOMI OSAKA
JAPAN TENNIS

Two-Time Major Champion

Naomi Osaka made her professional debut at the age of 16, earning rave reviews as she dispatched former U.S. Open champion Samantha Stosur and alerted the tennis world that she was going to be someone to keep an eye on in the coming years.

Within 2 years of joining the professional ranks, Osaka had crashed the top 50 in the world rankings and in 2018 she grabbed her first WTA title in Indian Wells, California.

Later that year, under the bright lights and heavy pressure of New York, the hard-serving Osaka used punishing groundstrokes to push 23-time major champion Serena Williams all over the court by beating her in straight sets to win the U.S. Open. In so doing, she became the first Japanese player to win a Grand Slam singles title.

Four months later, and 14 time zones away from where Osaka rocked the tennis landscape, Osaka played a gritty two weeks of tennis in sweltering heat—surviving four three-set matches— on her way to winning the Australian Open for another major title.

The win propelled Osaka to the top spot in the world rankings at that time and earned her the distinction of

MODEL BEHAVIOR

Osaka's father watched Venus and Serena Williams explode onto the tennis scene in the late 1990s and was inspired to teach the sport to Osaka and her sister Mari just like Richard Williams did with his daughters. Despite no knowledge of the sport, he coached Naomi for several years before she began getting professional instruction as a teenager.

being the first Asian player to hold that coveted rank. She also became the first player since Hall of Famer Jennifer Capriati did so back in 2001 to win her first two Grand Slam titles consecutively.

Naomi Osaka, known for being shy off the court, plays attacking tennis on the court, making her a serious threat to win an Olympic medal in Tokyo.

YOU'VE GOT MAIL

After Osaka's U.S. Open win she received a letter from Serena Williams, apologizing for her behavior in the final. During the match, chair umpire Carlos Ramos issued three on-court violations to Williams. Williams recognized how special the moment is to win your first major title and shared with media that it broke her heart to have ruined Osaka's moment.

ADAM PEATY
GREAT BRITAIN SWIMMING

Expected to Dominate Breaststroke Sprint Events

There is no question that Adam Peaty had a terrific 2016 Olympics in Rio de Janeiro. He won the gold medal in the 100-meter breaststroke, his specialty. This was the first medal of the Games for Great Britain. No British man had won an Olympic swimming medal of any kind for 24 years. Peaty also broke his own world record in the event twice during those Games. For good measure, he added a silver medal by swimming the breaststroke leg for Great Britain in the men's 4x100-meter medley relay.

As well as things went in Brazil at the Rio Games, Great Britain and Peaty expect even better from the 2020 Games in Tokyo. Peaty has lowered the 100 meters record twice since Rio. He is now both the first man to swim the distance under 58 seconds and under 57 seconds—he swam 56.88 in July 2019 at the World Championships in South Korea. This was Peaty's third straight World Championship in the event. He has recorded the 18 fastest times in the history of the event.

The IOC has added the 50-meter breaststroke as an event beginning in 2020. As it happens, Peaty is

PROJECT 56

Only Peaty has ever swum the 100-meter breaststroke in under 58 seconds. That was in 2016, and it kicked off what he called Project 56. He set a goal to be the first to swim the distance in under 57 seconds, which he did at the 2019 World Championships. His time of 56.88 seconds is nearly two and a half percent better than the next fastest time ever swam.

also the world record holder in that event. He has set this record four times and is the first person to swim the distance in under 26 seconds (25.95).

Given his dominance in these two events since 2015, at minimum a double gold celebration is expected for Peaty at the 2020 Tokyo Olympics. Anything less would surely be viewed as a disappointment from the defending world and Olympic champion.

"When I was 15, I almost hated racing in finals because I was so nervous. But as I got more experienced, I had to choose between fight or flight, and I've fought every time."

– Adam Peaty

TEDDY RINER
FRANCE JUDO

Two-Time Olympic Gold Medalist May Be Best Ever

Anyone planning to get their hands on an Olympic gold medal in the men's judo heavyweight class will likely have to take down France's Teddy Riner to do so.

In recent years that task has bordered on the impossible.

The 6-foot 8-inch Riner, arguably his country's most beloved athlete, hasn't lost a match since way back in 2010. The 144-match winning streak he has strung together is one of the most impressive runs in all of sports.

Riner is the two-time defending Olympic champion, having won gold at the 2016 Rio Games and the 2012 London Games, to go along with the bronze medal he won in his Olympic debut as a 19-year-old at the 2008 Beijing Games.

His skills are breathtaking to watch. Blending a lethal combination of speed, strength, and agility, Riner simply has no weaknesses that others can even consider attacking.

Riner has collected eight World Championships, his first in 2007 and his eighth in 2017. His win in 2007 as an 18-year-old, in which he defeated 2000 Olympic champion Kosei Inoue of Japan in the semifinals, made him the youngest ever

FLAG BEARER

When the delegation of French athletes entered the Maracanã Stadium in Rio de Janeiro, Brazil, during the opening ceremonies of the 2016 Summer Olympics, Teddy Riner was at the head of the pack as the flag bearer for his country. He said he was honored and proud to have been chosen to carry his country's flag while walking among so many great athletes.

world champion. He has also won five European Championships.

Riner skipped the 2018 and 2019 World Championships, instead choosing to direct all his focus on conquering the field for another Olympic gold medal at the 2020 Tokyo Games.

Judging by Teddy Riner's performances in the past two Olympics, and the past decade, chances appear strong that he'll be atop the medal podium once again in Tokyo.

ORDER OF MERIT

Riner was awarded the prestigious National Order of Merit in 2016. The President of the French Republic gives the award, created by former French President Charles de Gaulle in 1963, to distinguished citizens. Others who have received the award are legendary actor and mime Marcel Marceau and actor and filmmaker Gérard Depardieu.

LIN SHAN
CHINA DIVING

Talented Teen Poised to Continue Gold Medal Run

China's dominance in women's diving at the Summer Olympics over the past few decades is staggering. It has won a gold medal in the 3-meter springboard the last eight straight Olympics and since the 1984 Summer Games in Los Angeles it has claimed seven of nine gold medals in the 10-meter platform event.

With the emergence of gifted teen diver Lin Shan, China is positioned to carry on that dominance for many years to come.

Lin showed off her arsenal of dives and her steely nerves at the 2018 Youth Olympic Games in Buenos Aires, Argentina, where she snatched gold medals in all three women's diving events.

Lin opened by winning the 10-meter platform, outscoring the second-place diver by more than 60 points. Forty-eight hours later, she led the 3-meter springboard competition from start to finish, racking up an impressive 505.50 points. No other competitor in the field broke the 450-point mark. Lin then teamed with Colombia's Daniel Restrepo to win the international mixed team event. They rallied from ninth place after the first rotation of dives to win gold by a slim 1.25 points.

The young diver showed that she is more than ready for the Olympic stage with her strong performance at the World Championships in Gwangju, South Korea, in 2019. Lin partnered with Yang Jian to claim a gold medal in the mixed team event.

That's good news for the Chinese diving team and bad news for the rest of the world that must face the talented Lin Shan.

MAKING A SPLASH

The mixed team diving event, where competitors dive from both the 3- and 10-meter heights, was introduced at the World Championships in 2015 in Kazan, Russia. China had never won the event in its brief existence until Lin Shan stepped on the board in 2019 in South Korea and teamed with Yang Jian to win gold rather comfortably with 416.65 points.

To see China's Lin Shan win gold in the women's 3-meter springboard final at the 2018 Youth Olympic Games, scan here.

KIYO SHIMIZU
JAPAN KARATE

Two-Time World Champion Wants Gold at Home

During her elementary school days, Japan's Kiyo Shimizu would follow her older brother into the local karate training hall, where she fell in love with the sport.

Now, as one of the sport's genuine stars, Shimizu has an entire country following her.

Shimizu may just stand five feet tall, but she's a giant in the world of karate, a new Olympic sport for the 2020 Tokyo Games.

Since 2014, Shimizu has been dynamic in kata (see sidebar), where her laser fast reflexes and ability to execute crisp, perfectly timed moves continue to shine in competition. She has been called the "queen of kata" in her home country for years.

Shimizu won her first World Championship in kata in 2014 in Germany and backed that performance up by winning the world title again in 2016 in Austria.

In 2018 at the World Championships in Madrid, Spain, Shimizu took home the silver medal.

At the Asian Games in 2018 Shimizu took out Macau's Sou Soi Lam 5–0 to win a gold medal in kata, the seventh straight time a Japanese woman has won gold since the sport was added to the Asian Games' line-up in 1994.

Shimizu also won gold at the 2017 World Games in Wrocław, Poland.

When the world's best in karate gather next summer, they will compete at Nippon Budokan, a beautiful indoor arena (built exclusively for martial arts tournaments) that sits in the heart of Tokyo.

And that's where Kiyo Shimizu hopes to fulfill a lifelong dream and win an Olympic gold medal with her country cheering her on.

DOUBLE DUTY: KUMITE AND KATA

Shimizu's best event is kata, one of two that will be on display during the upcoming Olympics. Kumite is one-on-one fights where opponents deliver punches and kicks while attempting to score points, and kata is where competitors perform solo moves as judges grade their performances for technique, power, speed, sharpness, accuracy, and concentration.

To watch Kiyo Shimizu compete against Hikaru Ono in the All Japan Karate Championship, scan here.

SARAH SJÖSTRÖM
SWEDEN SWIMMING

World Record Holder in Four Events

Sarah Sjöström's journey to greatness got off to a rather slow Olympic start, which is ironic considering she's one of the fastest and most-decorated swimmers in the world today.

Sjöström finished in 27th place in the 100-meter butterfly in her Olympic debut at the 2008 Beijing Games, where she celebrated her 15th birthday during the Games. Four years later at the 2012 London Games she swam in four individual events but took home no medals, coming fourth in the 100-meter butterfly, in which she held the world record.

Sjöström strung together several years' worth of great swims leading up to the 2016 Olympics, including at the 2015 World Championships, where she eclipsed Dana Vollmer's time to reclaim her world record in the 100-meter fly on her way to winning the world title in that event for the third time.

When the Rio Games arrived, Sjöström was ready. She unleashed a powerful swim in the semifinals to break the Olympic record in

the 100-meter butterfly, and she returned to capture gold in the finals to become the first woman from Sweden to win swimming gold. She also won silver in 200-meter freestyle and bronze in 100-meter freestyle, becoming just the second woman in history to win medals in those three events at a single Olympic Games.

Leading into 2020, Sjöström is the world record holder in all four of the 50- and 100-meter freestyles and butterflies. She is on the fast track to becoming one of the greatest swimmers of all time.

EUROPEAN EXCELLENCE

At the 2018 European Championships, Sjöström added four gold medals to her ever-growing tally, winning the 50- and 100-meter freestyle and the 50- and 100-meter fly. She became the only woman in history to win those four events at a single meet, and it boosted her record medal total to 23 (14 gold, 6 silver, and 3 bronze).

To watch Sweden's Sarah Sjöström win the 100-meter butterfly at the 2016 Summer Olympics in Rio, scan here.

KERRI WALSH JENNINGS &
BROOKE SWEAT
USA BEACH VOLLEYBALL

Veteran Superstar Takes One Last Shot at Glory

Kerri Walsh Jennings is a legend in the sport of beach volleyball. The Californian is a three-time Olympic champion and four-time medalist. Walsh Jennings won three straight gold medals in 2004, 2008, and 2012 with her playing partner Misty May-Treanor. At the 2016 Rio Games, she and her partner April Ross won a bronze medal. For the 2020 Games, she plans to partner with Brooke Sweat, who played with a different partner in Rio. Walsh Jennings will be 41 years old come the 2020 Tokyo Olympics, relatively old for any athlete at this level.

Walsh Jennings has nothing left to prove in her sport. No one has won more matches. No one has earned more prize money. She and May Treanor once won 112 straight matches on the Association of Volleyball Professionals (AVP) Tour. Walsh Jennings won three straight World Championships (2003, 2005, and 2007) as well as three straight Olympic gold medals.

Brooke Sweat

With all of these accomplishments, the question of why Walsh Jennings is doing this is an obvious one. For Sweat, it represents a chance at Olympic gold that she hasn't won. For Walsh Jennings, why work so hard to grind out an Olympic berth to face the likes

The Summer Olympics: Athletes to Watch

DIGGING HER DEFENSE

One of the main reasons Walsh Jennings chose to partner with Sweat is because of Sweat's defensive skills. Walsh Jennings is fearsome at the net (she is 6-feet 3-inches tall), crushing big spikes and blocking shots and Sweat is a perfect counterpart, being a four-time AVP Defensive Player of the Year who specializes in digging balls headed for the sand.

of Brazilian stars Duda and Ágatha or 2019 world champion Canadians Sarah Pavan and Melissa Humana-Paredes? Walsh Jennings simply could not reconcile having her Olympic career end on what she felt was a poor performance. "I know what I'm focused on. I know very clearly what I want", Walsh Jennings said.

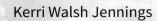

Kerri Walsh Jennings

"I can do it. The fire is there. I have a new partner. My sixth and final Olympics. I want this. I'm all in."
– Kerri Walsh Jennings

SHAUN WHITE
USA SKATEBOARDING

Winter Olympic Megastar Eyes First Summer Games

Shaun White—four-time Olympian, three-time gold medalist, and widely regarded as the greatest snowboarder of all time—may be back in the Olympics much sooner than expected.

Only this time minus all the winter gear.

And on a skateboard.

That's right, the first U.S. male athlete to medal three times in the same event at the Winter Games—he had a trio of gold medal wins in the half-pipe in Turin, Italy, in 2006; Vancouver, Canada, in 2010; and Pyeongchang, South Korea in 2018— spent time after Pyeongchang honing his significant skateboarding skills for a run at a spot on the U.S. squad as skateboarding makes its Summer Olympic debut in the 2020 Tokyo Games.

White has had plenty of success on a skateboard, too. He has earned five medals in skateboarding at the Summer X Games, which included capturing gold medals in 2007 and 2011. He won 18 medals at the Winter X Games, including 13 gold.

At the age of seven, White was discovered by legendary skateboarder Tony Hawk at a local skate park near San Diego. He turned pro in

VEERING FROM VERT

White's X Games success has come in vertical skateboarding, often referred to as "vert," where competitors ride up and down a ramp while performing tricks. At the 2020 Olympics, only the park (hollowed-out course with dome-shaped bowls and curves) and street (course featuring stairs, handrails, curbs, benches, walls, and slopes) events will be contested.

skateboarding at 17 (he turned pro in snowboarding at 13) and began riding for Hawk's Birdhouse Skateboards team. White will be 33 at the 2020 Tokyo Games.

White competed at the 2019 skateboarding World Championships in Brazil before deciding if competing in the Summer Olympics was a realistic goal. Judging by his ability to step up in the big moments throughout his career, the presence of the "Flying Tomato" in Tokyo was never in doubt.

BIG HEART

Throughout his career White has devoted his time and money to helping children in need. He works closely with St. Jude Children's Research Hospital, as well as the Boys & Girls Club and Target House. White has also worked with the Make-A-Wish Foundation where he has met with numerous families with children who are dealing with life-threatening illnesses.

KATIE ZAFERES
USA TRIATHLON

Dominant Triathlete Favored to Win Gold

Katie Hursey was a distance runner at Syracuse University when she made a decision that would change her life forever. She was recruited to join the USA Triathlon program and chose to move to Colorado for training. There she met her husband, triathlete Tommy Zaferes, who she would marry in 2015. She also discovered a passion for the physically demanding sport.

Zaferes found success in her first year of triathlon competition, earning USA Triathlon's Elite Rookie of the Year honors in 2013. She improved year over year, building to the 2016 Olympics in Rio de Janeiro. In 2015, Zaferes was second or third in six of eight events. Just before Rio, she won her first World Triathlon Series (WTS) race, and it looked like she had a real chance at a medal. Then Rio came and went. Zaferes finished a disappointing 18th.

Zaferes began her journey to redemption as soon as she returned home. Her coach identified an issue with her cycling training, which they corrected, allowing Zaferes to continue to improve. In 2017, she finished third in the International Triathlon Union standings, which determine the world champion.

TREAT YOURSELF

As a world-class athlete, Zaferes is rigorous about what and how much she eats. She does, however, have a tradition she sticks to that started when she was just a kid. It came from her dad, who always told her, "No matter if you win or lose, how you perform, make sure you go get ice cream." So Zaferes does after every competition (plus a burger too!).

In 2018, she was second, and in 2019, Zaferes won four of the first six events on the way to becoming world champion.

Zaferes' greatest competition at the 2020 Tokyo Games may well be from her teammates Summer Rappaport and Taylor Spivey. The trio swept the podium in a WTS event in May 2019 at Yokohama, Japan, where Zaferes won the race.

"The races that have shaped me the most are the ones in which I have felt dissatisfied. They are the ones that I learn the most from, they are the ones that motivate me to be better and they are the ones that produce a clarity of purpose in moving forward. As an athlete, I consider myself to be evolving. Each of these races and experiences aids that evolution."
– Katie Zaferes

GAME CHANGING EVENTS

MELBOURNE, AUSTRALIA

Seven countries boycotted these games, including the Netherlands, Switzerland, and Spain. These three were protesting Soviet military action in Hungary, a conflict that played out in competition. The IOC allowed the Soviets to compete, and in water polo they played Hungary in a semifinal match that turned violent. "Blood in the Water" screamed the headlines. Hungary won and went on to claim gold.

LONDON, UK

After six years of World War II, the world looked to war-ravaged London to pull off the first Olympics since 1936 (Germany and Japan were banned). It was not easy. These were dubbed the Austerity Games in a London that was broke. No new stadiums were built, and food was rationed, but the Games themselves were a huge success.

MUNICH, GERMANY

The 1972 Munich Games were marred by an attack on the Olympic Village. Palestinian terrorists killed two Israeli athletes and took nine others hostage. The drama played out on live television around the world. A botched rescue attempt 20 hours later left all nine Israeli hostages and five of the terrorists dead.

The Summer Olympics: Athletes to Watch

POLITICS...CRISIS...SOCIAL CHANGE

MOSCOW, USSR

In December of 1979, Soviet troops attacked the Afghan capital of Kabul, executed president Hafizullah Amin and made Babrak Karmal, who was a Soviet supporter, the new leader. This kicked off what would become a 10-year occupation. The United States led the idea of boycotting the Games if the Soviets did not withdraw, and ultimately more than 60 countries decided not to send athletes to Moscow.

MONTREAL, CANADA

Twenty-two African nations boycotted the 1976 Montreal Games at the last minute when the IOC allowed New Zealand to participate after having sent its rugby team to play in South Africa. The South African government was the subject of international scorn and sanctions due to its policy of racial segregation called apartheid.

RIO DE JANEIRO, BRAZIL

The IOC allowed 10 athletes without a country to participate under the Olympic flag. Amidst a worldwide refugee crisis, the IOC funded the training for the selected athletes. Examples of what they had survived include the Syrian Civil War and tribal genocide in the Democratic Republic of the Congo.

RESEARCH PROJECTS

Major moments on the world stage have impacted the Olympics through the years. The Research Projects below will bring a deeper perspective to these moments and the events that shaped them.

1. Research and detail the sequence of events from the time the terrorists at the 1972 Munich Games broke into the Olympic Village to the time the standoff ended at the airport. Why did the standoff end in tragedy?

2. At the 2016 Rio Games, members of the Refugee Olympic Team came from the Democratic Republic of the Congo (DRC). Research the situation in the DRC, going back as far as the Kivu conflict, and including Kasai region violence and the tribal violence between the Banunu and Batende peoples. Outline how this has become a humanitarian crisis, what is being done to help stop it, and what the human toll has been to date.

3. Research the 1956 Hungarian Revolution. What were the two sides? How did it end? How did it impact that year's Olympic Games in Melbourne?

4. What steps did the British government and the London organizers have to take to put the 1948 Games together? Make a bullet point list of the necessary measures from government loans to whale meat.

5. The Summer Olympic Games have been cancelled three times since their current inception in 1896. All three times the cause was the outbreak of a World War. The 1916 Berlin Games, 1940 Tokyo Games, and 1944 London Games never took place. Using poster board and plenty of images, construct a timeline of the major events that caused the Germans to start WWI and WWII.

OLYMPIC GLOSSARY OF KEY TERMS

archery—the sport of shooting arrows with a bow.

banned—to prohibit, especially by legal means.

compete—to strive consciously or unconsciously for an objective (such as position, profit, or a prize).

decathlon—an athletic contest consisting of ten different track and field events.

doping—the use of a substance (such as an anabolic steroid or erythropoietin) or technique (such as blood doping) to illegally improve athletic performance.

equestrian—of, relating to, or featuring horseback riding.

heat—one of several preliminary contests held to eliminate less competent contenders.

host city—the city that is selected to be the primary location for Olympic ceremonies and events.

hurdle—a light barrier that competitors must leap over in races.

medal—a piece of metal often resembling a coin and having a stamped design that is issued to commemorate a person or event or awarded for excellence or achievement; may also mean to win a medal.

nationality—a legal relationship involving allegiance on the part of an individual and usually protection on the part of the state.

opponent—a contestant that you are matched against.

participant—a person who takes part in something.

preliminary—a minor match preceding the main event.

pommel horse—a gymnastics apparatus for swinging and balancing feats that consists of a padded rectangular or cylindrical form with two handgrips called pommels on the top and that is supported in a horizontal position above the floor.

qualify—meet the required standard.

referee—the official in a sport who is expected to ensure fair play.

repechage—a race (especially in rowing) in which runners-up in the eliminating heats compete for a place in the final race.

spectator—one who looks on or watches.

sportsmanship—fairness, honesty, and courtesy in following the rules of a game.

stamina—enduring strength and energy.

standings—an ordered listing of scores or results showing the relative positions of competitors (individuals or teams) in an event.

substitute—a player or competitor that takes the place of another.

torch—a cylindrical or cone-shaped object in which the Olympic flame is ceremonially carried.

vault—to execute a leap using the hands or a pole.

venue—the place where any event or action is held.

victory—a successful ending of a struggle or contest; a win.

EDUCATIONAL VIDEO LINKS

Simone Biles: http://x-qr.net/1Jao
Sebastian Brendel: http://x-qr.net/1LFW
Caeleb Dressel: http://x-qr.net/1LAP
Allyson Felix: http://x-qr.net/1KYU
Janja Garnbret: http://x-qr.net/1Kax
Jason Kenny: http://x-qr.net/1L8t
Takeru Kitazono: http://x-qr.net/1KSu
Kliment Kolesnikov: http://x-qr.net/1JeS
Mariya Lasitskene: http://x-qr.net/1M9R
Sarah Sjostrom: http://x-qr.net/1LBP
Lin Shan: http://x-qr.net/1JEC
Kiyo Shimizu: http://x-qr.net/1KZ0

FURTHER READING

Blackaby, Susan. *G.O.A.T. - Simone Biles: Making the Case for the Greatest of All Time*. New York, NY: Sterling Children's Books, 2019.

Fitzpatrick, Jim. *Shaun White (The World's Greatest Athletes)*. North Mankato, MN: The Child's World, Inc. 2014.

Sabino, Elliot. *Tokyo 2020 Olympics: Know What to Say, How to Behave & Where to Stay*. Amazon Digital Services LLC. 2017.

INTERNET RESOURCES

https://www.olympic.org/sports
The website for the International Olympic Committee (IOC). Acting as a catalyst for collaboration between all parties of the Olympic family, from the National Olympic Committees (NOCs), the International Sports Federations (IFs), the athletes, the Organizing Committees for the Olympic Games (OCOGs), to The Olympic Partners (TOP), broadcast partners, and United Nations agencies, the International Olympic Committee shepherds success through a wide range of programs and projects.

https://www.teamusa.org
The official website of the United States Olympic & Paralympic Committee, celebrating and empowering Team USA Athletes. This site publishes the latest news and videos of USA athletes on the rise, heading for the Olympic and Paralympic Games.

https://tokyo2020.org/en/
The official website of the Tokyo Organizing Committee of the Olympic and Paralympic Games. Visitors will find information about the events, schedules, venues, opening and closing ceremonies, mascots, medals, emblems, the 2020 Torch Relay, and much more.

INDEX

The Summer Olympics: Athletes to Watch

PHOTO CREDITS

Shutterstock.com: Eastimages: 7, kovop58: 9, CP DC Press: 14, katacarix: 22, laszloambrus: 42, Mai Groves: 66, Hans Christiansson: 70, Leonard Zhukovsky: 73

Flickr: Marc: 32, JD Lasica: 34, Fido: 66

Dreamstime.com: Droopydogajna: 38, Bruno Rosa: 64, Peter Kim: 68

Wikimedia Commons: Fernando Frazão/Agência Brasil: 12, 44, 56, Tasnim News Agency: 16, Whatsup6624: 18, Pierre-Yves Beaudouin: 20, Sander van Ginkel: 24, jenaragon94: 26, 46, 50, Simon Legner: 28, Kirstin Scholtz: 30, Sandro Halank: 36, 40, Erik van Leeuwen: 48, Nardisoero: 52, Peter Menzel: 54, XIIIfromTOKYO: 58, Mauricio V. Genta: 60, Martin Rulsch: 62, National Media Museum from UK: 72, Thaler Tamas: 72, High Contrast: 72, Dewet: 73, NFYFLY: 73

All background images provided by Shutterstock and Dreamstime

AUTHOR BIOGRAPHIES

GREG BACH is the author of 10 books, including titles on sports and coaching. Growing up in Swartz Creek, Michigan, he has been a lifelong fan of the Detroit Tigers and has fond memories of attending games with his family at the old Tiger Stadium. He is a proud graduate of Michigan State University and resides in West Palm Beach, Florida.

SCOTT MCDONALD was a high school athlete in West Monroe, Louisiana, before serving 4 years in the U.S. Navy as a gunner's mate. He began his writing career at Richland College in Dallas, Texas, and went on to the University of Texas at Austin, where he majored in journalism. McDonald covered sports for high school and small colleges at *The Dallas Morning News*. He served as the managing editor of a newspaper near Austin and as publisher at another newspaper in Texas. He has covered sports for 20 years and he has covered Olympians and Paralympians since 2009. The Texas High School Coaches Association named him the State Sportswriter of the Year in 2014.